Ellie the Treasure Hun

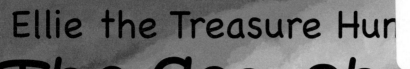

The Search for

By Linda C. St. Peter

Illustrated by Fiona Fuller

ISBN: 979-8-9885866-1-6

This book is dedicated to my granddaughter, Ellie.

Grandma is visiting. Ellie is thinking about treasure.
"Grandma," Ellie says. "X marks the spot."
"X marks the spot?" Grandma asks.

"Yes, X is where the treasure is." Ellie explains.

"Let's go treasure hunting. Come on Grandma" and Ellie takes Grandma's hand. Ellie has binoculars.

Grandma and Ellie walk down a dirt road outside Ellie's house. Ellie walks bent over studying the ground.

"It is called Old Dirt Road" explains Ellie holding her arms out wide, "because it is an old dirt road!"

Ellie and Grandma laugh. Grandma looks up and see the sign. It says "Old Dirt Road".

Ellie bends over again searching the ground. "Look for the X Grandma that is where the treasure is." Down the Old Dirt Road they walk.

Suddenly Ellie stops. "Look Grandma, X marks the spot!" Ellie points, "There Grandma! There!

Grandma looks and sees two little sticks laying across each other. They look like an X.

"We have to dig here" says Ellie. Ellie finds a bigger stick and starts to dig a hole under the X. But, the ground is hard.

"How far are you going to dig?" asks Grandma. "If we keep digging we will find the center of the Earth and the treasure. Ellie explains.

"Hmmm" says Grandma. "If we dig a big hole in the middle of Old Dirt Road what will happen to the cars driving on the road?"

Off of Old Dirt Road they search. "Look!" Ellie shouts and she points at a sparkling pink stone. "It is treasure!"

Grandma bends over and looks at the stone. "Wow" she says, "that is beautiful. I think it is a rose quartz."

Ellie picks up the stone and holds it up to see it sparkle in the sunshine.

Grandma hugs Ellie. "you are my treasure Ellie and I keep you in my heart."

Grandma makes an X over her heart.

Ellie takes Grandma's hand and they walk home.

Made in United States
Troutdale, OR
07/21/2024

21241023R00017